Camping in the Temple of the Sun

Camping in the Temple of the Sun

By Deborah Gould • Illustrated by Diane Paterson

Bradbury Press • New York

Maxwell Macmillan Canada • *Toronto*
Maxwell Macmillan International
New York • Oxford • Singapore • Sydney

10 9 8 7 6 5 4 3 2 1
The text of this book is set in Cheltenham Book. The illustrations are rendered in watercolor.

Library of Congress Cataloging-in-Publication Data   Gould, Deborah.   Camping in the temple of the sun / by Deborah Gould ; illustrated by Diane Paterson.—1st ed.   p.   cm.   Summary: A family's first camping trip is full of fun and adventure despite a series of mishaps. ISBN 0-02-736355-4 [1. Camping—Fiction.] I. Paterson, Diane ill. II. Title.   PZ7.G723Cam 1991   [Fic]—dc20   91-16358

For Steve and all he knows about the earth and sky

—D.G.

For my husband, John

—D.P.

On the carpeted floor of the big camping store, Jeannie crawled out of a large purple tent and on into a small green one. Billy, the baby, crawled behind her and Dad behind him. Gazing up in the dim green light, Dad said, "Well, it's cozy."

"Too cozy," Mom said, peeking in. "We'd never fit four sleeping bags in here."

Jeannie nodded.

"True," said Dad, handing Billy out to Mom. They went on searching for a tent that was right for a family of four on their first camping trip. Jeannie wondered how they ever would decide. Then she found the orange and yellow dome tent, and they all sat smiling in its warm gold light.

Mom said, "Let's buy this one," and Dad named it the Temple of the Sun.

At home with their package of folded-up tent parts, Mom said, "We'd better put it all together once and check it out before the trip."

Dad spread out the pieces and directions in the living room. Together he and Jeannie set up the tent on the rug. Inside it smelled new and rich with the promise of adventure. There they sat leafing through the *Campers' Guidebook* and decided on a trip to Great Rock Park.

"This will be a weekend trip—just two nights of camping. After that, maybe we'll try a longer one," said Mom.

They set out on a Friday afternoon, and the traffic made them later than they planned in reaching Great Rock Park. At the entrance they signed up for campsite #112 and found it in the fading sunset light.

"We'd better get the tent up before dark," said Mom, who was busy changing Billy. Dad and Jeannie worked together, as they had at home, but everything was harder now. Here they had strong wind and bumpy ground.

Dad said, "Ooops, I should have brought a hammer. We'll need something to pound these pegs and keep the tent in place."

While they laid out the metal frame, wind billowed through the fabric and sent it tumbling away. Jeannie chased and caught it. While Dad helped her untangle it, the frame toppled over.

"Where's Mom? We need her help!" said Dad.

Jeannie pointed at Mom, coming toward them. She held up a hammer. "I borrowed this from campsite #108," she said.

Keeping Billy in the backpack, Mom helped them finish fast. Entering the tent, Jeannie could smell earth and grass. Damp and dark in evening's shadow—this was different from the way it felt at home or in the store.

While they were eating supper at the picnic table, Dad said, "Tonight at eight the park rangers have a program at the outdoor theater. Let's walk down there after supper."

"Fine, but I smell rain. We should take both umbrellas," said Mom. Before they set out, she sent Jeannie over to campsite #108 with the hammer and a bag of popcorn.

A large camping van was parked there. A tall, friendly-looking girl hopped out. "Hi, I'm Sandra. Thanks," she said, taking the hammer and the popcorn. "The rest of my family is at the ranger show; I just came back for my poncho," she explained.

"Come with us," said Jeannie, wanting to be with Sandra more.

At the theater the ranger announced, "Tonight's program is Wildlife at Great Rock." A drizzle had started, but people stayed, watching from under rain gear and umbrellas. As the ranger was telling them how dangerous the bears could be, a downpour began. "That's all, folks," the dripping ranger said.

Jeannie ran ahead through the rain with her new friend Sandra, who asked her to come over for breakfast in the morning.

Mom, Dad, Jeannie, and Billy dried off with towels inside the tent. Dad held Billy on his lap and read some picture books by flashlight. He said the words louder as the rain beat harder on the tent. Mom and Jeannie sat on their sleeping bags and read their own books by flashlight.

Billy looked sleepy, but he wouldn't go to sleep. First he was silly, then cranky, and his diaper was full. Rain was coming down harder than ever, so Dad changed Billy's diaper in the tent. That made the whole tent smelly. Mom stuffed the diaper in a plastic bag and ran out to the garbage through the rain.

Billy fussed more, and Dad began singing. Mom and Jeannie joined him, to rise above the rain. They sang every song that Billy liked, beginning with the fast ones. They went on to the slow ones and at last the lullabies. Finally Billy was asleep. "I'm sleepy now myself," said Mom, wriggling into her bag.

"I'm exhausted," said Dad, wriggling into his.

Jeannie got into her sleeping bag, but she couldn't get comfortable. She needed to pee. She thought about the bathroom building that seemed far off through the rain. She thought about the bears that might be out there in the dark. That made her shiver and have to pee more.

Finally she nudged Mom. "Please come with me to the bathroom," she whispered desperately.

"All right," said Mom. "Take your soap and toothbrush. At least we'll get to wash up." They slipped out of the tent, opened an umbrella, and hurried toward the light of the long stone bathroom building.

In the women's bathroom, two teenage girls were blow-drying their hair. Another, wearing a Walkman, brushed her teeth. After rinsing, she told the others, "The weather says rain all day tomorrow."

"Ugh," said her friends. "Yuck."

"Ugh and yuck," said Mom.

"What will we do in the rain tomorrow?" asked Jeannie on their way back under the umbrella.

"Museums, sight-seeing, indoor games . . . We'll be all right," said Mom.

The tent seemed damp inside, but at least the sleeping bag felt cozy. Jeannie quickly fell asleep. She woke again to Billy babbling, Mom saying "hush." She slept and woke again to Billy whimpering, Dad saying "shush." She slept again and woke to morning light and rain.

While Jeannie's family ate their breakfast in the car, Jeannie joined Sandra's family. Sandra's dad was grilling bacon in a little cooking corner of the van. He made hot cereal and hot chocolate, too.

"We're going on to White Springs Park this morning," Sandra said as though she wished she could stay.

Jeannie had never thought that Sandra would be gone so soon. After breakfast and good-byes, she walked sadly to her campsite.

Billy's toys were strewn all over the tent. Jeannie had to play there with him while Mom and Dad cleaned out the car.

"What will we do now?" asked Jeannie grumpily.

"We'll drive around the park and get some scenic views," said Dad.

"Then we'll visit the nature museum and have lunch at a restaurant outside the park," said Mom.

The scenic views were blurred by rain, but the nature museum was fun. Jeannie got to hold a snake and watch an owl up very close. They ate in a restaurant with a fireplace. Dessert was warm homemade peach pie.

"Not bad, so far, for a rainy day," Dad said after lunch.

Mom said, *"But*, if it doesn't clear by four o'clock, I think that we should pack our tent and stay at a motel tonight."

"But Mom . . . ," said Jeannie.

"Let's not give up so fast," said Dad.

"I don't want another rainy night stuck in the tent, and I'll bet Billy doesn't either. At a motel, we'd be comfortable and dry. We would have reading lights, TV, maybe a swimming pool. We can camp another time."

Jeannie thought Mom was right, but still she hoped the sky would clear by four.

On the way back Billy fell asleep in the car seat. Mom stayed in the car and read while Dad and Jeannie brought a box of board games to the tent. After several rounds of Candyland, Jeannie looked up. The patter of rain had stopped. A bright, warm light came through.

Jeannie and Dad stepped out into sunshine. By the car, Mom and Billy watched the sky, where gray was quickly giving way to blue.

"Forget about motels. Let's climb that mountain trail we passed this morning," said Mom.

Hiking the trail was an adventure. They saw chipmunks, sleek red newts, yellow finches, and other little animals—no sign of any bear. They reached a lookout tower, and by then the view was clear in all directions.

Back at the tent, they changed into bathing suits. There was just time for a sunset swim.

For supper they grilled hamburgers and roasted marshmallows. Afterward Dad gazed up at the clear night sky. He pointed out constellations among the stars. He called them "star animals" and seemed to have a story about each one. He promised to tell "a great bear story" when Jeannie was ready for bed.

While Mom and Jeannie were in the women's bathroom, they saw the teenager with the Walkman. "The weather says sunny all day tomorrow," she told her friends.

"Great," said the friends.

"Great," said Mom and Jeannie. Linking arms, they walked beneath the starry sky, back to Dad and Billy in the Temple of the Sun.